Be Careful What You Wish For

Lynn Ann Post

Internet addresses given in this book were accurate at the time it went to press.

Printed in the United States of America
Published in Hellertown, PA

Library of Congress 2021905278
ISBN 978-1-952481-14-7

2 4 6 8 10 9 7 5 3 1 paperback

This book is dedicated to my family, who always encouraged and believed in me.

To my friends, who always lent an ear and offered ideas and advice.

However, this book was written for my students. When I started the journey, of teaching writing, I thought I would be educating my students.

But in return, I realized that from their ideas and stories, they were educating me. They inspired me to write this book, and for that I am truly grateful:

Cameron A., Ian B., Braden B., John B., Amiee B., Harley B., Brooke C., Roman C., Sofia F., Jacob G., Ashley H., Brielyn H., Ella Rose K., Mason K., Tyler M., Milania M., Alexander P., Madelyn R., Kaitlyn S., John S., Dean T., Christopher W., Jacob W., Olivia W., Mason W., Naomee A., Ian A., Cole A., Thomas B., Ethan B., Christian C., Xavier C., Torin C., Damien C., Julia D., Isaac E., Dominic E., Gracie F., Jake H., Mena K., Zachary K., Karah L., Caroline M., Braeden M., Kennedi P., Dominic R., Jack S., Collin W., and Morgan Y.

A special thank you to Katie Dawe for the beautiful cover artwork and to Deb Matz for all her help.

Chapter 1

Extraordinary... *meaning very unusual or remarkable.* That is how Sardinia Louise Kingstree described herself in one word. Sardinia Louise Kingstree, or Silk for short, was a very unique and adventurous young lady, not because of her raven black uncombed hair, which greatly contrasted against her snowy white skin, nor because of her daily mixed-matched attire, but because of her extra creative imagination and her love for adventure.

If you were to ask Silk to describe herself in more than one word, she would simply blurt out, without hesitation: a dreamer, an artist, an actress, adventurous, and somewhat **bizarre...** *meaning very strange or unusual.* Others, excluding her only friend, Kayla, would describe Silk as sort of spacy, unfocused, a daydreamer, or just plain old different, but a great best friend. No matter what others said or thought about Silk or the way she dressed or acted, she just pretended that she didn't care. She just wanted to be left alone, and that was all.

One of Silk's favorite things to do each week was to make up a schedule of special wishes or adventures for each day, Monday through Saturday, and live out those wishes through daydreams while sitting alone in her dark bedroom closet or her backyard treehouse. Sundays were spent with family, and later in the afternoon she would finalize the next week's adventures in her journal. Some wishes took her to amazing places and different times in history, like a princess living in a huge stone castle in Medieval Europe or a queen living near the ancient Egyptian pyramids. Her wishes were special to her and allowed her to be who she really deep down desired to be.

As soon as Silk got home from school, she would hightail it to either her bedroom closet or her treehouse, situated in the oversized oak tree, where no one bothered her. Each week, when she wrote her wishes in her journal, the same opening page greeted her. Written in bold purple letters was, "Be careful what you wish for." Her mother had said those words to her numerous times. Her mother often questioned her on why she chose to be by herself in a fantasy world instead of riding her bike or hanging out with Kayla. You know: normal kid stuff. Silk never gave the questions much thought and purposely avoided answering her mom. Her beloved journal captured her experiences from the special places she visited and what she had learned.

It was now Sunday evening and Silk was in her private treehouse with her private journal, trying to decide where her adventures would take her in the week ahead. She thought about it long and hard.

"Let's see," she mumbled to herself. "How about I become a professional basketball player in the WNBA?" She carefully wrote her wish under the bold printed *Monday* in her private journal. Now for

Tuesday, she thought, *What if I could become the first female astronaut to walk on the moon?* Again, she carefully wrote in her, yes, private journal.

Without pausing, she quickly continued. Wednesday's wish would be infinite youth for her family and her. Wow! Imagine never aging! If this wish could happen, then her Grandma Virginia would still be alive! She would have been able to climb up to the treehouse and sway freely on the long, braided rope swing with her, never having to worry about her aching joints again. As she thought about her grandmother, she brushed away a few tears from her eyes and realized just how much fun that would have been. Silk continued working on her remaining wishes while stuffing a pretzel into her mouth.

Thursday's wish would be to see what it would be like to be invisible. Silk chuckled under her breath just thinking about the things she could do with Thursday's wish and how much fun it would be to play tricks on unsuspecting people.

Friday's wish made her begin to wonder what it would be like to have all the money in the world. The thoughts that sprung into her mind were endless! Again, she carefully wrote in her journal and got even more excited for the upcoming week's adventures. After stuffing another pretzel into her mouth and taking a quick sip of her orange soda, she penciled in "Saturday." This wish would take a little more thought and planning because she would only have time for a short adventure. On Saturday, Kayla was having a big birthday party, and Silk wanted to be totally there for that. That meant there would be no daydreaming during the party...maybe.

"So, Saturday. Let me see," she whispered to herself, while running her fingers through her already **disheveled**... *meaning messy* hair. "Hmmm, what if there was a world with no bullying, and everyone would always be happy?" That would be outstanding because, even though she acted like she didn't care what others thought or said about her, it would be really nice for everyone to accept her for who she was instead of avoiding her like she had a contagious disease! "Why can't everyone be happy, too?" she mumbled. "Without bullying, everyone could be happy."

Satisfied with her entries for the week, Silk tucked her journal neatly into her pants pocket and made her way out of the treehouse and  back to her house. Once back in her room, Silk carefully hid her journal under her purple flowered pillow, laid down, and fell asleep.

Chapter 2

Silk blasted out of bed like a lightning bolt just before her Garfield alarm clock was set to ring at 6:30 AM. She jumped up and sprinted to the shower. She washed her hair but never dried or thoroughly combed it, because it just didn't matter to her. Silk grabbed a pair of blue plaid pants and an orange flowered t-shirt from her dresser and quickly got dressed, not worrying if it even matched. She quickly brushed her teeth and breezed down the stairs into the kitchen to grab a banana, a sip of orange juice, her lunch, and her backpack. She kissed her mom goodbye as she bounded out the backdoor and headed for school.

Silk speed walked the two blocks to school. She was always in a hurry to get there early so she could have some private time to think and to plan her adventure for when she got home. Try as she might to concentrate at school, sometimes she would drift off into one of her adventures during class, which irritated her teacher, Mrs. Dyer.

Mrs. Dyer understood Sardinia and appreciated her imagination, but knew she had her hands full keeping her focused during class. So, in order to keep Sardinia on task and to keep her eyes off the classroom clock, she would frequently call on her. **Ironically**... *meaning oddly, unexpected, or* *strange*, most times Sardinia gave spot-on responses to the questions and was never embarrassed if she didn't know an answer. She would just politely apologize to Mrs. Dyer and continue doing what she had been doing before being called on.

As the school buzzer sounded at the end of the day, Silk was already sprinting down the three flights of stairs and out the back door. As she bolted past Kayla, she smiled and chirped, "Call ya later." Heading straight to her bedroom closet, after grabbing a quick brownie her mom had just baked, she **careened**... *meaning rushed or raced quickly,* into the cramped, dark space to begin her adventure.

"A WNBA basketball player…," Silk whispered to herself. Her heart fluttered, and she began thinking about all the hard work she would have to put in

each day at practice and all the fun she would have with the other players. The sweetest thing about the whole deal would be getting paid for something that she already loved to do! In the real world, Silk was not very good at basketball, but she always wondered what it would be like if she was. This had to be the best wish ever. She leaned back into her fuzzy brown pillow and closed her eyes. She could picture the locker room and her name, "Kingstree," on a jersey hanging on the locker door. She heard all the excitement in the locker room as her teammates dressed for the big championship game, and the **exuberance**... *meaning excitement or being full of energy*, coming from the anxious fans in the packed arena.

Running out onto the basketball court she had a feeling of butterflies in her stomach. There was an adrenaline rush like the one she'd had back when her dad took her whitewater rafting for the first time. The buzzer shrieked, and the game began. Both teams battled up and down the court. With Silk's team leading only by 2 at the half, she assumed the coach wouldn't give her any playing time because she was a rookie, and it was a close game.

However, while in the locker room, the assistant coach announced the names of the players resuming the court. "Arndt, Walters, Marquarth, Brown, and Kingstree," bellowed the assistant coach. "Let's bring the championship home, ladies!" Silk's teammates all yelled in unison.

Silk was incredibly nervous, but it was her big chance. She knew she had to give it her best.

Silk started to wonder, "What if I mess up? What if we lose because of me? What would all of the fans think?"

At that point, she really didn't know if she could take the pressure of being a professional athlete.

The team jogged back onto the arena court. Once the game resumed, Silk forgot about her nerves, and the adrenaline kicked in. With seven seconds left in the fourth period, her team was now down 74 to 73. The ball was passed to Silk down court. She grabbed the ball in midair and was totally knocked off her feet by a player from the opposing team. Silk was now going to have to take the two foul shots, which was not her strength. Once again, her stress level started to **hinder**... *meaning to create difficulties,* her concentration on the important task at hand.

The official threw Silk the ball. Her hands were sweaty and shaking. All she could hear was her heart pounding in her chest. She knew she needed to make these next two shots. She reached up and shot the first shot. Swoosh! She scored. The fans went crazy, and Sardinia began breathing a little easier.

Now the second shot. Silk gently tossed the ball. It hit the backboard and circled the rim. Her heart was pounding as the ball circled for what felt like a lifetime. Then, finally, the ball found the center of the net and fell through.

There were three seconds left in the game. Silk's team needed to get the ball back or keep the opposing team from scoring. A player from the other team threw the ball toward one of their teammates. The ball hit her foot and **ricocheted**... *meaning to rebound off of a surface*, and went right to Silk. The look on her face was pure panic. She focused and dribbled around until the buzzer rang out.

They had won the game and the championship. The crowd went crazy, and Silk felt like she was on top of the world.

"Sardinia!" Silk heard her mom yell from the bottom of the stairs. "You need to come down for dinner."

She felt relieved at her mom's beckoning, grabbed her journal, and quickly jotted down some notes about her experience as a WNBA basketball player.

She came to the conclusion that way of life wouldn't be for her. Even though she would have been famous and wealthy, she hated stress and would have felt terrible disappointing her teammates, the fans, and mostly herself if she would have messed up.

Being a WNBA player wouldn't be much fun for me, Silk thought. *I think I just like being Sardinia Louise Kingstree, and that's all.*

Silk finished her journal entry and raced down the stairs to the smell of meatloaf and mashed potatoes. She found her mom in the kitchen at the **helm**... *meaning in control.*

Silk set the table and told her mom and dad all about making the foul shots and winning the basketball championship, but she told them that it was just not right for her.

Her mom and dad lovingly looked at each other and smiled. They enjoyed hearing about her daily adventures and never got a word in edgewise when she was talking. However, both of her parents wished she would soon grow out of this regular routine because she was getting older.

After shoveling down two plates of meatloaf and mashed potatoes with gravy, Silk cleared the table and grabbed her phone to call Kayla.

"Hey, Kay," Sardinia piped. "I just found out what it would be like to be a WNBA basketball player! It was not all that it is cracked up to be, and the stress level was unbelievable. It was just not for me."

"Are you going to find time Saturday to come to my birthday bash?" Kayla asked, changing the subject. "Please tell me you are coming and that you won't be daydreaming at my party," she begged. "My mom has so much planned for my birthday, and I want my bestie to enjoy it with me."

"I wouldn't miss it for the world!" Silk responded. "I promise, no daydreams."

Chapter 3

Silk slept like a baby Monday night. She was excited to jump up before her alarm clock announced, "Wake up sleepy head!" She quickly washed up and did her daily morning ritual. Afterward, she bounced down the stairs to the kitchen where her mom had made buttermilk pancakes and mini sausages. Silk snagged a pancake, wrapped two sausages in it, and grabbed her things to head off to school.

"Bye, Mom," she mumbled with a mouthful as she rapidly closed the door.

The school day seemed like it would never end. Silk was worried because she wasn't sure how she had done on the Social Studies test she'd forgotten to study for. She would find out tomorrow and prayed she had done okay.

After Silk got home, she inhaled another homemade brownie while she ran up the stairs to her closet. Settling down on her fluffy pillow, she could finally imagine herself being lifted into space.

Silk was going to be the first woman astronaut to walk on the moon. What a great honor it would be. She pictured herself speaking at conferences, schools, and other **venues**... *meaning places where things happen.* As the rocket ship prepared for liftoff, Silk felt a surge of adrenaline and nerves.

"2...1...0...All engines running. Liftoff! We have liftoff, 29 minutes past the hour. Liftoff on Eternity 7... Tower is cleared!"

The first thing Silk felt was the hard thrust forward in her seat as the first stage of the rocket ship released. Thankfully, she was held in place by very broad, nylon straps. Minutes later, the second stage erupted, and she was slammed back into her seat by the sudden force of the **acceleration**... *meaning a vehicle's capacity to gain speed within a short time.* Once out of the Earth's gravity, Silk and the other two astronauts were weightless, and it felt like she was floating alongside the stars. What an uplifting feeling.

Silk detested the sensation of her stomach rising into her throat, which had already happened twice, and it was starting to make her sick. Silk knew that before becoming an astronaut she would be put through a preparation regiment of tests. She realized right then that she would never be able to do it. Silk decided to cut her wish short without even getting close enough to step on the moon.

Silk knew that being the first woman to walk on the moon wasn't for her. She breathed a sigh of relief and jotted her experience in her journal. She was happy being herself for now, Sardinia Louise Kingstree.

Chapter 4

On Wednesday in Social Studies class, Silk held her breath as Mrs. Dyer handed back the tests. Her paper was handed back face down, and she knew that wasn't a good sign.

Slowly she turned the test around... a 71 percent. A "*C!*"

Mrs. Dyer had written a note in red ink that said, "Just think what you could have scored if you would have paid closer attention. I am disappointed and hope you are better prepared for next week's test."

Silk knew her parents wouldn't be happy, but it wasn't like she was failing. She still had an "A" average.

Just then, Kayla threw a crumpled-up paper at Silk to get her attention.

"What did you get?" she mouthed.

Silk formed a "C," with her fingers and shrugged her shoulders, not looking back at Kayla.

The rest of the day seemed to last forever. After school, Kayla caught up with Silk and asked her how she could have possibly gotten that grade. Kayla once again suggested to Silk that she stop daydreaming in class.

"You are my best friend, and I really care about you," Kayla said. "But it is getting old now. A lot of the other kids and teachers are concerned about you."

"I don't care what everyone thinks!" Silk blurted with tears in her eyes. "I have to get home."

Silk stopped at the front door to wipe the tears from her face. Then she tiptoed up the stairs, bypassing her mom in the dining room.

"I need to show Mom my test," Silk mumbled to herself. By the time Silk opened her bedroom door, her mom was already standing right outside in the hallway. She had a concerned look on her face.

"Are you okay?" her mom asked. "I noticed that you had been crying as you came into the house."

Sardinia told her mom that she had forgotten to study for her Social Studies test and gotten a "C," but that she still had an "A" average in her class.

"I really think you have been more distracted lately, and you also have been spending too much time alone in your closet," her mom suggested in a gentle, caring voice.

Silk listened to her mom and understood what she was saying. But it is hard to change something that you have been doing for years. Her mom got up from her bed and straightened the fluffy purple comforter.

"I think you were more bothered by this grade than I was. Maybe it is a good lesson for you. Come on down and have some freshly baked sugar cookies when you are ready."

After some sugar cookies and two glasses of milk, Silk called Kayla and apologized for her behavior. "I'm sorry for the way I acted today after school.

You're right about me daydreaming, but it's hard to stop. I'll try."

"I'll see you tomorrow, Silk," Kayla said. "You didn't owe me an apology. I knew you were upset, and I thought I could help."

Chapter 5

In school Thursday, Silk tried tremendously hard to pay close attention to Mrs. Dyer. She even stacked her books up on the corner of her desk so she could not see the clock as easily. Mrs. Dyer noticed Sardinia's efforts and gave her a wink and a smile. Silk felt good about her focus, but she still could not wait to get home.

As she ran home, she **pondered...** *meaning thinking about something before making a decision,* about her wish for today. It was for her family and her to live forever as they were. That would be amazing.

Running back into the house after school and grabbing an apple and a bottle of water, Silk headed outside to her treehouse. She could once again see Grandma Virginia and her swinging high above the hedges in the backyard. She laughed to herself as the picture in her mind came to life.

Silk thought long and hard about "living forever." She started to think about negative things that could **arise...** *meaning something that could emerge,* from her and her family always staying the way they were, but no one else.

What if Kayla got older, but she never did? Silk realized that while she and her family would stay the way they were, everyone else would get older and die.

"I really wouldn't want to see all my friends waste away or get older, because I would miss them," she stammered to herself out loud.

Silk also wondered if living forever and staying as she was would get boring. Would you get tired of it?

She loved her grandparents the way they were and how they had shared their experiences, wisdom, and stories with her. She loved when her Grandmother Virginia had hugged her when she was sick and made her milkshakes to make her feel better. This wish could be very difficult.

Silk quickly reached for her journal and wrote, "I can't do this. I think I am just happy being Sardinia Louise Kingstree and keeping things just the way they already are."

As Silk was putting away her journal, she again wiped tears from her eyes and smiled as she pictured her Grandma Virginia

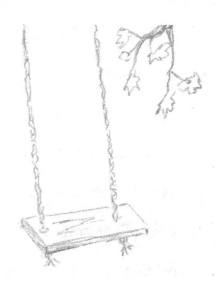

grinning from ear to ear flying on the rope swing. She realized that her imagination, along with her memories of her family, were all she needed.

However, Silk could not turn off her mind. The wish had her feeling uncomfortable. She went downstairs to the kitchen to talk to her mom, who was preparing for dinner.

"What's up, honey?" Sardinia's mom asked.

"It was my wish tonight," Sardinia responded.

"What wish was that?" her mom asked.

"My wish was for our family to live forever like we are now, and it upset me," Sardinia mumbled quietly. "I imagined Grandma Virginia on my rope swing in the backyard having a ball. I could hear her laughing, and I enjoyed what I saw."

"Then why are you so bothered?" her mom questioned.

"I also realized that my friends will get old and die, and I wouldn't like that at all," Sardinia sobbed.

"I understand why that would bother you," her mom answered in a calming voice. "I guess that's why our lives are so precious. You do the best you can while you are alive because everyone will get older. That is just another part of life."

After a few minutes in deep thought Silk piped, "I think I am happy just being 12 and myself, Sardinia Louise Kingstree."

Silk walked up to her room still feeling upset, but not wanting it to show on her face, she tried to smile and called Kayla.

"What's up, Silk?" Kayla answered.

"I just needed someone to talk to and thought I'd call you," replied Silk.

"You sound upset. What's going on?" Kayla asked.

"Well, it was about the wish that I thought about today. It has me very confused and upset."

"What wish was that?" Kayla spouted, sounding a little annoyed.

"It was for my family and me to live forever the way we are right now," Silk answered.

"That's foolish. Why would you want something like that?" Kayla wondered. "I wish you would stop doing this every day. There's just no reason for it. You get yourself so caught up in these situations for no reason. One of these days, I'd like to take a look at your adventure journal to see just where my best friend goes all the time."

Silk listened to Kayla for quite a while and finally admitted that maybe there was no reason for her daily adventures, except that she had done them for so long that it was part of who she was. Still, she wasn't sure if she was comfortable having someone else reading her deepest thoughts.

"I think that the time has come to stop this silliness and find NORMAL things to do to occupy your time," Kayla added. "I love you, Silk. You are my bestie, but sometimes I wonder about you, and I really worry."

"You are probably right. I'll try," Silk mumbled. "See you tomorrow."

As Silk hung up the phone, she realized that maybe her parents and Kayla were on to something, but how could she stop now? She would have to give this a lot of thought, especially because tomorrow's wish—being invisible—was going to be so much fun.

Chapter 6

Friday morning came quickly. Silk was awakened when she heard someone pounding on her bedroom door.

"Sardinia, honey, are you up?" her mom yelled.

"Yeah," she answered while rubbing the sleep from her eyes.

Thank heavens her mom had looked at the time, because Silk didn't remember getting into bed. Then she realized that she hadn't even changed into her PJs or set her alarm. She had fallen asleep after writing in her journal and falling off into deep thought.

Silk rushed to get ready for school, jumped down the stairs two at a time, and grabbed a peanut butter covered rice cake from her mom's hand.

She gave her mom a quick thank-you kiss, snagged her backpack, and burst out the door. As she ran toward school, she also remembered that school photos were being taken today. She quickly scanned her outfit—blue jeans and a pink T-shirt with "*AWESOME*," written across the front in gold letters. "Good enough," Silk mumbled to herself. Actually, the outfit she had thrown on today was probably the most normal looking one she had worn in quite a while.

"Hey Silk, hurry up, or we're gonna be late!" Kayla beckoned. "I was worried when I got here and didn't see you, especially after our conversation last night. Are you okay?"

"Yeah, I just overslept. Let's get to class," Silk quickly replied, focused on the classroom door where Mrs. Dyer was glaring.

"Good morning, ladies," Mrs. Dyer greeted them.

"Good morning, ma'am," both girls answered in **unison...** *meaning to answer at the same time.*

Right after coming in the door and finding their seats the morning bell **blared...** *meaning really loud.* Silk had never been this close to being late before, and her heart was racing. She would make sure from now on to double check that her alarm was set. She was jarred out of her train of thought when

Mrs. Dyer announced that today she would be introducing a new writing activity.

"Girls and boys, today we are going to use our imaginations for a new way of solving writer's block," she continued while looking right at Sardinia. "You will be timed for five minutes and be asked to write down anything that comes into your mind. Don't worry about neatness, spelling, or punctuation, just try to write down as much as you can in the timeframe I give you. To help you out, I will play some music. Start writing whatever comes into your mind. No one will read this but you."

"Well, I guess we are all going to be the guinea pigs today," Lena whispered from behind Silk. Lena was a good student, but she loved things her way so Silk knew this would be a challenge for her.

"This could be my lucky day," Silk muttered under her breath. "I love to write, and everyone knows I have quite an imagination."

Each student was handed a new tan journal with their names written across the front in red marker. Silk knew Mrs. Dyer had done them all because she had beautiful cursive writing and was a stickler about neatness and correct letter formation.

"I will be starting the music. No laughing or looking around the room. Just write anything that comes to your mind. Ready?" Mrs. Dyer finished as she popped in a CD.

The music sounded like a combination of nature sounds and Mozart. It was very relaxing although Kole, one of the quiet boys in class, started to giggle to himself. He was immediately squashed as Mrs. Dyer gave him her, "don't do it," look.

The five minutes went by fast, and then Mrs. Dyer bellowed, "STOP! Look at how much you have written. Raise your hand if you wrote more than one full page."

Silk glanced around the class. Every hand was waving in the air. Mrs. Dyer had a big SUCCESS smile on her face. She seemed really pleased and so were a lot of Silk's peers. Some of the kids in class hated writing and had trouble thinking about what to write and were really amazed at how easy this had been.

Silk quickly glanced down at her journal and realized that she had filled three and a half journal pages. Her penmanship wasn't even that bad. She was surprised and felt a tremendous sense of pride in her work.

Mrs. Dyer might be on to something here, Silk thought.

From behind, once again, Silk heard Lena mumble, "Wow, I can't believe I wrote all of this without planning it out first. That was amazing."

Lena was a very organized, perfectionist at whatever she did and so not being able to plan out this activity took her way out of her comfort zone.

"Now I would like each one of you to take some of those ideas you have written in your journals and write a short story for homework tonight," Mrs. Dyer said. I will be the only one reading it, so make sure it is appropriate," she finished with a smile glancing at Kole.

I was really looking forward to this homework assignment, but I was also focused on my 'being invisible' wish, too, Silk thought. *I guess I'll have to split my time in half tonight.*

As Silk was leaving class, Mrs. Dyer beckoned her over to her desk with her pointing finger.

"Sardinia, I was very elated with your focus and interest today in class," she beamed. "I knew this assignment would be right up your alley with your imagination. I can't wait to read your writing tomorrow. I really think you could be an inspiration to some of the others in this class."

"Thank you, ma'am. I'm really trying. Today was really fun. See you tomorrow," Sardinia replied and then she made her way out of the classroom.

Throwing her backpack on her bed, Silk grabbed her wish journal and headed for the closet **anxious** ... *meaning excited*, to dive into her into her next adventure.

Flopping onto her fuzzy pillow, Silk laid there for a while thinking about the writing assignment she had been asked to complete. She decided to tackle her assignment before her daily wish.

Rereading her jumble of words from the writing activity in class today, she realized that she had actually written about her wish for today, probably because it had been on her mind all morning. She decided she could combine her writing assignment and wish together into a story for Mrs. Dyer. She smiled about the **coincidence**... *meaning a* *remarkable happening when events or circumstances happen by accident or chance.*

Silk decided that she would write her story first in her tan journal from Mrs. Dyer, and she would later enter her reflections of the adventure in her wish journal.

"Where should I start?" she muttered to herself. She laughed out loud as she thought about a normal day and then adding being invisible for a day. "I guess I wouldn't have to shower or wash my hair in the morning, and I could go to school in my PJs," she giggled, thinking about being able to do whatever she wanted to do and not get caught. Even going downstairs in the morning for breakfast would be funny, especially when she would take a muffin from her mom, kiss her cheek, and say, "Thanks."

Silk imagined the surprised expression her mom would have on her face and probably scream. *I guess I could just take the muffin and sneak out!* Silk thought.

On her way to school, she noticed the paperboy delivering the papers. She decided to have some fun. As the young boy threw each paper on a neighbor's doorstep, Silk ran ahead and threw it back. She could hardly contain her laughter after the first two papers **haphazardly...** *meaning marked by a lack of order or direction*, flew in the air right back to the paperboy. He stood there for a while and finally dropped his bag full of papers, running down Butztown Road, yelling something about a ghost. By this time Silk was laughing so loud that Mr. Dilliard, the neighbor down the street who was bending down working in his garden, stood up and asked, "What's so funny?"

He stood up, expecting to join in on the laughter, when his face became a series of wrinkled lines that **encompassed** ... *meaning have or hold within,* a very puzzled look on it. He took off his glasses, wiped them on his shirt, put them back on, and stood there bewildered. As Silk tiptoed past him, she heard him say to himself, "My goodness, maybe I really do need to get my ears checked like the wife said."

This was just too much fun, Silk thought to herself, although she would have to be very careful at school because so many people knew her voice and her laugh. Nearing the school, Silk saw Kayla leaning up against the playground fence, waiting for her.

Should I just tell her? Silk questioned herself. *I don't want her to get mad at me.* She decided to let Kayla in on the deal but decided to have a little fun first.

Carefully Silk bent over and picked up Kayla's backpack, which was lying on the grass next to her. Kayla did not notice at first because she was focused on her phone. Slowly, Silk walked in front of Kayla carrying the backpack. At first Kayla just stood there and then suspiciously looked around the school grounds muttering, "Okay, what's going on?"

Kayla hadn't really responded like Silk thought she would have. "Come on, let me in on the joke," Kayla continued.

Silk leaned close to Kayla's ear and whispered, "It's just me, Kayla."

"Silk, where are you? What's going on? This isn't funny! You're freaking me out!" Kayla cried.

Not wanting to upset Kayla anymore, Silk cleared her throat and spoke to Kayla. "You can't see me right now because I'm invisible. Don't ask me how because I don't know. You're the only one who knows."

"Sardinia Louise Kingstree, this is the worst joke ever!" Kayla screamed.

"Please keep your voice down," Silk pleaded.

"This isn't funny," Kayla said. "You're going to get yourself in trouble! I'm going to class. Good luck."

Kayla grabbed her backpack from Silk's invisible hand.

Wow, I really didn't think Kayla would be so upset, Silk thought. *Maybe I shouldn't have made this wish.*

Once inside the classroom, Silk noticed Kayla glancing frequently back at her seat. Silk knew Kayla couldn't see her, but Kayla was still in disbelief.

Mrs. Dyer also glanced at Sardinia's desk and asked Kayla if she was sick. Kayla told Mrs. Dyer that she did not know, and immediately glanced Silk's way, wearing an I-told-you-so smile.

"That's fine, Kayla. I'll have the office call her house later," Mrs. Dyer answered as she continued her roll call. "I'm sure there must be a good reason she isn't here today. She had a perfect attendance going for a chance to win a new bike at the end of the year."

Silk had forgotten about the Attendance Recognition Award her chance to win a bike that she had been working so hard to get.

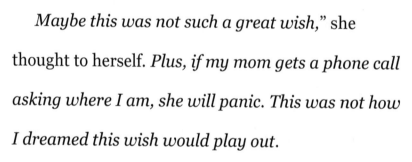

Maybe this was not such a great wish," she thought to herself. *Plus, if my mom gets a phone call asking where I am, she will panic. This was not how I dreamed this wish would play out.*

Suddenly, Lena jumped up from her seat behind Silk and blurted to Mrs. Dyer, "I just heard Sardinia. She must be here somewhere!"

Silk must have spoken aloud without realizing it!

Mrs. Dyer looked up over the top of her glasses, scanned the empty seat in front of Lena, and told her to sit down and stop interrupting the class.

Silk chuckled silently and saw Kayla shake her head. She then decided to walk home when class broke for lunch because she was starving and knew she couldn't carry a tray back to her seat without causing a ruckus.

Being invisible isn't as much fun as I thought it would be, Silk thought to herself. *I could've gotten myself in a lot of trouble with people I care about, and I also could have lost out on a chance to win a new bike. I guess it's just better being who I am— Sardinia Louise Kingstree.*

After Silk finished writing her story for Mrs. Dyer in her journal, she **reiterated**... *meaning to say* *something again,* her conclusion about why being invisible was not for her and filled in her daily entry in her own journal.

As Silk closed her journal, she smiled to herself. She felt very confident about her short story and hoped Mrs. Dyer would like it, too. She could hardly sleep that night and couldn't wait for school the next day.

Chapter 7

"Wake up, Sleepy Head," Silk's her alarm clock shouted. She was shocked that she hadn't been up before her alarm went off. She had a rough time trying to fall asleep last night because of the excitement of wanting to share her story with Mrs. Dyer. This was the same feeling she always had the night before Christmas with all the anticipation of seeing what gifts were under the tree.

Silk ran to the bathroom, showered, brushed her teeth, and got dressed. Of course, she did not tackle brushing her hair—because she thought it looked just fine.

"Sardinia, what do you want for breakfast?" her mom yelled up the stairs.

"I'll just have a banana, Mom," Silk replied.

Jumping down the stairs, two at a time, she took the banana from her mom, grabbed everything else she needed, and headed off to school. As Silk rushed to school eating her banana, she briefly remembered her wish for tonight: all the money in the world.

She had almost forgotten about her daily wish because she had been so excited about her writing assignment. This wish was a tough one, and she knew it could have a downside, but she had all night to think about it. Right now, her focus was on handing in her assignment and finding out how Mrs.

Dyer liked it. *Who knows*, she thought to herself. *Maybe Mrs. Dyer will share it with the class.*

When Kayla and Silk finally arrived at the classroom, the room was a buzz. Everyone was talking about their stories. An unusual excitement filled the room. Mrs. Dyer stood by her desk with her hands folded in front of her green button-down sweater with the biggest smile ever.

"Okay, girls and boys, I hope all this excitement is about your stories. I couldn't wait to come to school today to see what you have all done. How many of you enjoyed doing this?" Mrs. Dyer questioned.

Almost all the hands in class went up, except for a few boys. They never liked any kind of homework. Mrs. Dyer just ignored them, making the comment, "Well I guess you just can't please everyone all the time. I cannot wait to hear your stories," she said. "Would anyone like to tell the class what theirs is about? We will not have the time today to hear everyone's story at length, but I would like to hear a few of your ideas. Any takers?"

A number of hands flew into the air, as Mrs. Dyer surveyed the willing. "Okay, Lena, what is your story about?" Mrs. Dyer prompted.

"My story is a sad one. It's about a soldier who has to go off to war and doesn't want to leave his new wife who he loves very much. The music you played made me feel sad, and that's what I pictured," Lena explained.

"Thanks, Lena, I can't wait to read it."

"Kayla, what is yours about?"

"My story is about a girl who finds out who she really is and what she has to offer others," Kayla explained, glancing back at me.

"Wow! Interesting, I am so excited," Mrs. Dyer beamed, almost jumping in place. "Sardinia? Would you like to share your story idea?"

Silk was excited. Everyone was looking at her. From behind, she felt a small finger jab her in the back.

"Go ahead," Lena whispered.

"Yes, ma'am," Silk answered. "My story's theme is about being invisible and realizing that it isn't as great as you thought it would be."

"Well, that really has me interested, Sardinia," Mrs. Dyer smiled. "Does anyone else in the class feel the same way I do?"

Silk glanced around the room and was amazed to see all her classmate's hands in the air, even Kole's.

"Well, Sardinia, would you be willing to share your story with the whole class or would you rather I read it myself later?" Mrs. Dyer asked.

This was the moment Silk had been waiting for. It was her time to show others just what she could do. Suddenly she felt unsure. Would they laugh at her? She told herself that she didn't care because it happened so often anyway, but laughing at her writing would hurt more. Writing was her world, her way of forgetting everything else and **encapsulating**... *meaning to express essential features of something,* herself into her own fantasy.

"Sardinia?" Mrs. Dyer beckoned once more, "Would you like to share your story?"

"Okay," Sardinia managed to reply, her hands shaking as she held her journal. As she read her story, you could have heard a pin drop. Everyone was listening to her every word.

It was a great feeling and when she had finished, to her surprise, everyone clapped. Mrs. Dyer walked over and gave her a big hug.

"That was terrific!" Mrs. Dyer squealed. "If this is any indication of what all of the other stories are going to be like, I will be elated! Maybe I am really onto something! I am so happy right now and can't wait to go home this evening and read all of your stories! If I find stories that are extraordinary, I might even enter them in a writing competition!"

The lunch bell rang, and Mrs. Dyer instructed the class to hand in their journals as they filed out of the classroom to lunch.

"Sardinia, I am so proud of you, maybe we have finally learned how to harness your imagination for some good writing," she chirped with a big smile. "I see great things in your future, maybe even a bike." Mrs. Dyer added a wink and a chuckle.

"Wow, Silk, I was very impressed with your story, but don't you ever try to pull that being invisible stuff on me for real," Kayla laughed. "What an imagination!"

"Thanks, but I wanted to ask you something. Was your story about me?" Silk inquired, with a concerned tone in her voice.

"Maybe," Kayla answered. "I wouldn't have to make a lot of it up though, would I?"

"Okay, but can I read it sometime? Maybe I can find out who I really am," Sardinia finished. Both girls laughed.

Silk was very interested in what Kayla had written, maybe it really could help her learn to be herself and not have to go off on her daily adventures. She sighed to herself as the girls entered the cafeteria.

"Hey, Silk," someone tapped her on the shoulder from behind. It was Elaine—a shy girl who stayed mostly to herself, but was always nice to everyone. "You are a great storyteller, I really enjoyed your story today. Maybe you can help me learn how to do what you do."

"Sure," Silk remarked, smiling back at Elaine.

"See what I told you, Silk. Be yourself and everyone will learn to see you for who you really are," Kayla quipped with an I-told-you-so smile.

Silk noticed that she could interact with others besides Kayla and felt like she was finally being accepted by her peers. Maybe her parents and Kayla were right, maybe she just needed to do "normal" things and start letting others get to know her. She knew she couldn't expect everyone she came in contact with to like her, but that she could handle. This was fun right now, and she felt great.

The day flew and she even walked home with a few kids from her class, which normally didn't happen.

"See ya tomorrow," Rebecca called out, another classmate who had never acknowledged her before.

"See ya," Silk yelled with a cheerful wave.

As she bolted through the front door, her mom was waiting.

"You had me worried," she said in a concerned voice. "You never get home this late. Are you okay?"

Sardinia could hardly hold back any longer, "I had the best day of my life!" she cried. "Everyone loved my story, Mrs. Dyer said she sees great things in my future, and all the kids talked to me at lunch, and I walked home with Rebecca, and she never talked to me before this, and..."

"Whoa, slow down," her mom stopped her by putting her hand over her mouth before she could ramble on. "What story?" her mom asked trying to take in the whole thing.

"Well, our assignment was to write a story from what we had written in our journals while Mrs. Dyer played music. I realized that I had written about my daily wish of being invisible! Everybody loved it and Elaine, that real shy girl in my class, asked me to help her learn how to write like I do! Can you believe it? I had the BEST day ever!" she rambled.

"I am so happy for you, but this is what we have been trying to tell you," her mom continued, "I am so proud of you and your newfound self-awareness."

"Mom, can you help me pick out an outfit tomorrow for Kayla's party and help me with my hair?" Silk asked, lovingly looking at her mom.

"I would be happy to help you, but I think you can handle that all by yourself. However, I will be happy to take a look at you before you leave if you'd like my input?" her mom replied with tears in her eyes.

"Thanks, Mom. I have to call Kayla," Silk yelled as she flew into the kitchen grabbing a granola bar and bopping up the stairs with her phone.

When Silk got to her room, she noticed her daily journal laying on her bed and realized that she had never once during her day given her wish a thought.

"I can't believe I went through a whole day without thinking about what I was going to write for my daily adventure," she mumbled to herself. "I must have been so consumed with all that happened today that I didn't have the time to let my mind wonder.

too."

"Hey, Kayla! What are you doing right now?" Silk asked when Kayla answered her phone.

"Actually, I just sat down to play Minecraft. Why?"

"Cool! Can I come over to play for a while?"

Kayla was silent for a few seconds. "Kayla, you there?" Silk questioned, not hearing anyone on the other end of the conversation.

"Yeah, I'm still here," Kayla finally answered.

"Well, can I come over?"

"Sure, but what about your daily wish thing?" Kayla answered, **perplexed...** *meaning very puzzled,* at Silk's sudden interest in coming over to her house to play.

"Oh that, I'll do it later. I'll be there in a few," Silk piped, already jumping off her bed and heading down the stairs with her phone in hand.

"Mom, I'm going next door to Kayla's for a while. Okay?"

"You're going where?" her mom questioned, shocked. Lost for words, her mom smiled and wondered if at last her daughter had expanded her daily horizons. Whatever the reason, her mom felt confident about the change in Sardinia and her newfound **persona**... *meaning the side of someone's character that is presented or perceived by others.*

"Hey, Kayla!" Silk hollered as she burst through the front screen door. "Where are you?"

"I'm in the den! And please stop yelling, my dad is sleeping," Kayla retorted.

"Sorry, I forgot your dad works nights," Silk replied, trying to keep her voice level somewhat **subdued**... *meaning quiet, thoughtful, and restrained.*

Finding it hard to keep quiet any longer, Kayla asked Silk, "I'm just curious why you came over to my house today. Did your mom kick you out?" she spouted **sarcastically**... *meaning implies an intentional taunting or ridiculing.* "You haven't been to my house in at least six months."

"I know. It's so weird," Silk said. "I had such a great day at school today. It made me take a long hard look at myself and realize that I'm more than I thought I was."

"What are you talking about?" Kayla replied a little taken aback.

"When Mrs. Dyer had us write that short story for school and then asked me to read mine to our entire class, I was nervous. I didn't want everyone to laugh at me," Silk explained. "But it didn't turn out like I thought it would. So many kids complimented me on my story, talked to me at lunch and after school, and Elaine even asked me to teach her how to write like I do."

Silk felt on top of the world while plopping onto the sofa.

"You know, Silk, I've been trying to get you to understand that for a long time. You're such a good friend and an incredible writer, but you spend so much time by yourself in that closet. I'm so happy you're here. I'd love to read your wish journal, I am sure it is fascinating!" she finished.

"Let's play," Silk exclaimed and both girls flopped down, side-by-side on the area carpet in front of the TV, giggling.

Sardinia and Kayla played Minecraft, Truth or Dare, and talked about the upcoming birthday party. They even tried on some clothing, which Kayla gave to Silk because it was too small for her, until it started getting dark outside.

"I have to get going, Kayla, but I had so much fun. Thanks for the clothes. See you tomorrow morning."

As Silk walked home, she felt like a different person. Why hadn't she listened to her parents and Kayla before this? All those days and nights where she felt alone and different. All this time she could have just taken pride in herself and allowed people to see her for who she was. She knew that not everyone would be her friend and not everyone would like her, but she could live with that. The weight of the world was off her shoulders. For once, she felt like she belonged.

"Sardinia!" Her mom beckoned from the front porch step, "Come on, honey, it's time for dinner."

After helping her mom clear the table and wash up the dishes, Sardinia went up to her room and looked through her closet to pick out an outfit for the next day. She decided that she was going to wear a jean skirt she had just gotten from Kayla, her yellow sweater, and a matching yellow headband. She was still excited and realized she had not entered her wish in her journal.

Silk sat on the side of her bed. She thought about having all the money in the world. *Wow! Having all the money in the world could be great.*

Silk put her arms under her pillow and closed her eyes. She thought about her mom never having to worry anymore about the bills and her dad not having to work and instead spending time gardening. Silk imagined her family buying their own house and not have to pay rent to their crabby landlord anymore. Maybe they could buy a house like the white Cape Cod house in a photo her mom had cut out and hung on the fridge. The house was from an issue of a *Better Homes & Gardens* magazine surrounded by a white picket fence crawling with roses. Silk remembered her mom say that it made her feel good to dream about having it one day—even though she knew it probably would never happen.

Silk laughed to herself, *I guess I am like my mom, fantasizing about things that could never happen.*

Fighting to stay awake, Silk **surmised...** *meaning a thought or idea based on little evidence,* that having all the money in the world could be a greedy wish, too. She thought, *If my family had all the money in the world, no one else could live. What a selfish wish this would be. The world would be poor.*

Writing in her journal, she scribbled that having all the money in the world would not work and how horrible it would be. "I guess we will just have to still deal with the crabby landlord, but we still have each other, and we are happy. I am just happy being me,

Sardinia Louise Kingstree, and keeping things the way they are."

Chapter 8

The bright sun woke Silk early Saturday morning.
She laid in her bed, thinking, reflecting on her week,
and smiling.

For once in her life, she felt free—like she could be
proud of who she was. Sliding her feet out from
underneath the covers and sitting up on the side of
her bed, she saw her reflection in the white, wooden,
oval mirror she had gotten from her grandmother
years ago. She realized that she was definitely
different from a few days ago. She still looked the

same, but her self-confidence had improved. She could do anything she wanted without feeling judged.

"Wow! Today is going to be the best!" Silk blurted out loud. Today was Kayla's party. Silk knew her whole class would be there, minus Julia, Kole, and Mason, who all had a soccer tournament.

Maybe they'll all see the new me, too, she thought to herself.

Giving her reflection a thumbs up she scrambled into the bathroom to take a shower.

Whistling as she came down the stairs into the kitchen, her parents smiled.

"Well, aren't we bubbly this morning," her dad remarked.

"I'm just really excited for today!" Silk responded, grabbing two pieces of French toast.

"What's so special about today, besides it being a weekend?" asked her dad.

"It's Kayla's big birthday bash!" she exclaimed.

"Well, that is special," he declared. "By the way, you look very lovely this morning. I don't think I have ever seen my little girl wear a skirt before," he finished, sipping his coffee.

"Now, dear," her mom broke in. "Sardinia feels good about herself, and it shows. She has had a great week and is realizing that she doesn't need to **seclude...** *meaning to keep away from other people,* herself in her room any longer. Her image of herself has changed."

Silk's mom gave her a quick kiss on the top of her head.

"You're right, Mom. I actually can't wait to go to Kayla's party and finally feel like I belong."

Remembering her recent conversation with Kayla, Silk asked her mom, "Do you think she would like my secret journal for her birthday?"

Not waiting for her mom to answer she sprinted off, ecstatic at her own suggestion.

"Do you really think Kayla is going to want your old journal?" her dad called after her from behind the morning paper. "I can take you to the store this morning if you'd like to get her something else."

"I think my journal will mean a lot to her," Silk chirped. "She asked me if she could read it. I think my journal will be the perfect gift."

As Silk sprinted up the stairs to grab her journal, she overheard her mom say to her dad: "I'm so proud of her. She is really growing up."

Before Silk wrapped the journal in her favorite purple starburst wrapping paper, she decided to finish up by writing in her last entry. Her wish for today was for a world with no bullying and that everyone could be happy all the time. The thought of this wish made Silk smile.

"Can you imagine if there were no more bullies, sorrow, or unhappiness?" she said to herself. Lying back on her pillow and again thinking about her week and her feelings, she knew it wouldn't last forever. She knew that there could never be just happiness. Things happen that make us sad.

Ridding the world of bullies would take a lot more people learning to stand up for themselves and others so bullies couldn't **prevail...** *meaning to reign victorious.*

This wish wasn't realistic because in order to always be happy, people would have to learn to appreciate what their life had to offer and to keep moving forward no matter what was **dealt...** *meaning to give to one as a share,* to them.

Silk thought, *I guess it's like Mom always says, "Your life is what you make it, and make sure you learn from your mistakes."*

Silk finished her journal entry by writing, "*I know now what I need to do: just be me, Sardinia Louise Kingstree.*"

On the last page she added, *"This journal is for my best friend who never gave up on me and helped me find myself, for this I am forever grateful. Love, Silk."*

Checking her hair and her outfit in the mirror, Silk headed down the stairs, wrapped journal in hand, to ask her mom to do a final **inspection...** *meaning to carefully inspect, or view.*

With a thumbs up from mom and dad, and quite a few pictures taken before she left, Sardinia headed for Kayla's house.

Chapter 9

As Silk was walking down the street to Kayla's house, she heard loud laughing and taunting. Turning the corner of Butztown and Steuben Roads, she saw where all the noise was radiating from.

She noticed Elaine, the quiet girl from school, circled by some older boys on bikes throwing a beautifully wrapped present with a large yellow bow back on forth over her head. Elaine was crying and begging them to stop. Without hesitation, Silk quickly set her gift on the sidewalk and ran toward the intolerance taking place. Yelling as she ran with her arms *flailing... meaning swinging wildly,* the perpetrators scattered, bikes whizzing everywhere.

Silk ran to Elaine's side and asked her if she was okay. Still crying uncontrollably, Elaine managed to nod her head yes.

"I am so sorry, Elaine," Silk replied, upset herself. She knew how Elaine felt being the victim and told her that from now on she needed to speak up for herself and not allow people to treat her poorly.

Silk picked up the torn, battered gift and handed it back to Elaine.

"Come on, let's get to the party," Silk consoled, now breathing a little easier.

"Thank you, Silk," Elaine finally spoke, "I didn't know what to do when those boys stole my present from me, and I couldn't get it back."

"Believe me, I know how you felt, it has happened to me many times," Silk responded compassionately. "but I have finally realized that we have to stand up for ourselves and not let others bully us. My mom says there is strength in numbers."

"Kayla's gift is all ripped. I can't take it like this," Elaine realized starting to sob again. "Maybe I should just go home."

"And let those boys win? I don't think so," Silk said. "Kayla will understand, and I'm sure she will love her gift, because it's from you." Sardinia paused. "Oh my, I just sounded like my mom." Both girls laughed.

When the girls reached Kayla's backyard, they could hardly believe their eyes. Colorful tents held games, crafts, and all types of food. A clown was making balloon animals. There was a tub for bobbing for apples, and even a dunk tank that featured Kayla's dad.

Kayla spotted Silk and Elaine. She came running. "Hey, guys! I'm so glad you're here! We're going to bob for apples!"

Kayla suddenly noticed that Elaine had been crying.

"Are you okay, Elaine? What happened?" she asked.

"Oh, it was nothing," Silk interrupted, not wanting to ruin Kayla's day.

"Some boys grabbed your gift on my way here and Silk rescued me," Elaine responded.

"Are you okay?" Kayla inquired. "Who were they?"

"We know who they were, and I don't think they will ever bother us again!" Sardinia **accentuated**... *meaning to make more noticeable.*

"You should have seen Silk, yelling at the top of her lungs and waving her arms like a crazy person," Elaine laughed. "I think she scared them off. But your gift got ripped."

"What does it matter? I tear the paper off anyway," Kayla smiled. "Let's go bob for apples."

As Elaine strolled into the party, Kayla grabbed Silk by the arm and smiled, "Thanks. You're the best."

Silk had a wonderful time at the party. She felt so relaxed that she even sang karaoke! After hours of games, fun activities, funnel cake and other numerous treats, all of Kayla's guests headed home. Silk offered to stay to help Kayla and her parents clean up.

"You really don't have to stay to help us," Kayla's mom reassured her. "We've got this."

"No, I really would like to help out," Silk said. "I just wanted to tell you what a great party this was. I really had the best time ever."

"You're very welcome, and thanks so much for your help," Kayla's mom responded as she picked the unraveled streamers off the neighboring shrubs.

"Silk!" Kayla yelled. "You told me to wait to open your gift. Can I open it now?"

"Sure!" Silk replied, "I hope you like it."

As Kayla opened the neatly wrapped box, she looked up at Silk with the biggest smile on her face. "Your private journal? Seriously?" she blubbered, elated. "Wow, this is the best gift ever!" With tears in her eyes, she embraced Silk and mumbled, "I feel very special knowing that you would share your most treasured writings and experiences with me. Now maybe you finally can be yourself and move on to bigger and better adventures," she finished.

"It is my pleasure! You've helped me find myself and never gave up on me. You're truly the best friend ever," Silk responded as she brushed a tear from her eye. Stepping back, she added, "I had the best time today at your party, and not once did I even think about not fitting in. I just did my thing and let everyone see me for who I am. Thanks."

"Sardinia!" Kayla's mom yelled. "Your mom just called and asked if you could come home right away."

"Oh, I didn't realize how late it was. I have to get home for dinner. See you tomorrow! Thanks again," she yelled as she ran up the street carrying the small trophy she had won for her karaoke performance.

Chapter 10

"What's up, Mom?" Sardinia asked as she came bursting into the house. "I'm sorry I'm late. I just lost track of the time," she continued, worried that she was in trouble.

"Sardinia, slow down," her mom interrupted. "You aren't in trouble. I just had a phone call from your teacher, Mrs. Dyer."

"What?" Silk sputtered, confused by the mention of a call from her teacher. "I don't understand. I didn't do anything wrong."

"I don't think she was calling to complain about anything in school. She sounded excited and just said that she had good news. I just wanted to let you know a couple days ago Mrs. Dyer called me telling me that your story was chosen to be published. I'm sorry; she asked me not to tell you. You are supposed to give her a call right away," her mom added. Here is her number."

A little confused and hesitant, Sardinia dialed the number written for her on the pink Post-it note.

"Hi Sardinia, I am so glad you called me back so quickly. I hope I did not interrupt your evening," Mrs. Dyer yelped with excitement in her tone.

"Uh, not really, but I am curious as to why you called me. Is it about the contest my mom just told me about?"

"I wanted to call you to give you and your family the exciting news!" Mrs. Dyer replied. "Do you remember the writing pieces we did a few days ago?" she inquired.

"Do you mean the story I wrote about being invisible?" Sardinia asked.

"Yes, yes, that's the piece I'm talking about," Mrs. Dyer sputtered. "You see, she continued, I submitted a few of the stories from our class to a writing competition, and yours was chosen to be published!" she calmly explained. "I am so excited for you and your writing future!"

"What?" Sardinia squeaked, amazed at what she had just heard.

"Sardinia, I am so proud of you and wanted to know if you and your family could come at about 7 a.m. before school tomorrow morning so I can explain to you and your parents what this honor involves if that is okay?" Mrs. Dyer **queried**... *meaning to ask someone a question.*

"Yeah, I guess we can," Sardinia rebutted. "Mom, my story won a writing contest, and Mrs. Dyer would like you and Dad go to school tomorrow morning to meet with her to discuss what's involved."

"How exciting!" her mom cried out. "Yes, yes, of course we can come."

"My mom said they will be there tomorrow morning, Sardinia responded, still trying to comprehend what was going on.

"Great! I'll see you in the morning!" Mrs. Dyer quipped, full of an **exhilarating**... *meaning making one feel very happy*, energy.

"Sardinia, aren't you excited?" her mom inquired wondering why her daughter was not bubbling over with cheer.

"Mom, I can't believe that my story won a writing contest!" Sardinia finally spoke, still not fully grasping the reality of such a great honor. "I wonder what happens now?" She ran for her phone. "I have to call Kayla!"

"Hey, Kayla, guess what just happened?" Sardinia gushed, now finally digesting the idea of winning a writing contest.

"What's up?" Kayla asked.

"I won a writing contest, and Mrs. Dyer wants my parents to come to school tomorrow to discuss what's involved with the contest! I'd like you to come along with us."

"I'm not surprised, Silk. You have an amazing talent. I'm so happy for you!" Kayla blurted, sounding very excited. "I can't wait to hear what you are going to win! You deserve to be noticed and taken seriously. See ya tomorrow." Kayla hung up before she could say anything more.

Chapter 11

Sardinia and Kayla raced down the hall to Mrs. Dyer's room.

"Hi, Mrs. Dyer," both girls yelled in **unison...** *meaning an action of speech together.*

"Well, hello, girls!" Mrs. Dyer piped, surprised by the enthusiastic welcome.

"Come on in Mr. and Mrs. Kingstree," Mrs. Dyer said, interrupting the girl's bliss.

"Sorry, Mom, we're just excited!" Sardinia bubbled, somewhat embarrassed. "Sorry, Mrs. Dyer," she continued.

"No need to apologize. I'm excited, too," Mrs. Dyer whispered to Sardinia as she walked past her to the front table to join her mom and dad.

"Would you like a cup of coffee, Mr. and Mrs. Kingstree?" Mrs. Dyer inquired. "I also have freshly baked oatmeal cookies."

"Yes, coffee and a cookie would be great!" Mrs. Kingstree said, anxious to get to the real reason for the visit.

"Do I get a prize or what?" Sardinia blurted. "This is so thrilling!"

"Sardinia!" her mom gasped. "Where are your manners?"

"I'm sorry, Mrs. Dyer," Sardinia muttered, embarrassed for her outburst.

"I am very excited, too, Sardinia," Mrs. Dyer replied reaching for her **satchel...** *meaning a bag carried on the shoulder with a long strap.*

"What happens now that Sardinia's story was chosen?" Mrs. Kingstree inquired as she sipped on her coffee.

"Well," Mrs. Dyer started, "I sent 12 of the best stories from my classroom to the Keystone Publishing Company's Contest for Young Writers that choses 100 young writers to be published in their annual book. These writing pieces have been chosen from thousands of entries in the United States. But before that happens, all of the winners and their families are invited to attend an award banquet with dinner and all."

"Where is the banquet being held, and when is it?" Mrs. Kingstree probed.

"The banquet is scheduled on Saturday, November 2nd at 7 PM, and I will also be going," Mrs. Dyer continued, "and it will be held in Washington, DC at the Walter E. Washington Convention Center. All hotel expenses and meals will be covered!"

"Wow! You're so lucky," Kayla shrieked, "I am so jealous, but I'm happy for you," she beamed while hugging Sardinia and stuffing an oatmeal cookie into her mouth at the same time.

"Now the really neat thing about that evening will be the announcement of the Grand Prize winner who has been selected from the top 100 student entries and judged by a panel of authors and publishers from across the United States."

"This is quite an honor. I have never had any of my students get chosen in my 32 years of teaching, so I'm elated!" Mrs. Dyer continued. "The Grand Prize is an all-expenses-paid trip for the author and their family to Disney World."

"But what about you? Don't you get to go with us Mrs. Dyer?" Silk asked.

"Yes, I am going. I'm also allowed to bring a guest. Also, the teacher of the winning student gets $500 and a year's worth of classroom supplies from various vendors," Mrs. Dyer beamed. "I would love that!"

"Well, this is all so overwhelming," Mrs. Kingstree commented, holding her hand over her chest.

Looking at Mr. Kingstree, she added, "You will have to ask off work to make sure you can attend the ceremony. Do you think they will let you off?"

"I don't think it will be a problem," Mr. Kingstree replied.

As Mrs. Dyer crunched on her oatmeal cookie, Silk hugged Kayla. They both giggled with excitement.

"Well, I better get myself ready for class," Mrs. Dyer announced, "Please sign this permission slip. I'll take care of everything else."

"November 2nd is only a month away. I can't wait," squealed Silk as both girls giggled with anticipation.

"I'm just as excited as Silk is," Mrs. Dyer said. "You have a very talented daughter, Mr. and Mrs.

Kingstree, and you should be very proud. I'll be in touch with you about upcoming information as soon as I know what is next," Mrs. Dyer continued as she wrote the date on the Smart Board to prepare for the day.

Chapter 12

As far as Silk, was concerned the month of October seemed like it lasted forever. Her grandmother, Virginia, would have said that something moving so slow was like molasses in January.

The only things that helped move the month along were all the compliments and well wishes from her peers, teachers, and even Mrs. Ashenfelder, the school custodian who always gave her an extra peanut butter bar when they had them in the cafeteria.

"Mom, do you think I will win the Grand Prize?" Silk asked her mom as she ate breakfast the day before leaving for the banquet.

"I think you stand as much of a chance as anyone, but I don't think that is the most important thing," her mom countered, beating the pancake mix.

"What do you mean?" Silk asked.

"Well, I think the most important thing is that you have been given a once in a lifetime opportunity that a lot of other students would jump at a chance to have. It's not just about winning; it's about knowing your story was chosen out of thousands of entries," her mom explained.

"Yeah, I guess I am very lucky," Silk mumbled, realizing that her mom was right.

Chapter 13

As the Kingstree's car wheeled into the parking lot at the Marriott Hotel, Sardinia started to get butterflies in her stomach. Her mind was racing with excitement. Mrs. Dyer was waving to them from the front entrance of the hotel.

"You should see how beautiful my room is," she exclaimed as the bellmen in gold and maroon suits unloaded the luggage from the Kingstree's trunk.

"Hi, Silk!" a voice came from behind Mrs. Dyer.

"Kayla, what are you doing here?" Silked yelped, already running to greet Kayla.

"Mrs. Dyer was told she could take a guest and she asked me. I asked my mom and dad, and they said it was fine. It was really hard not being able to tell you, but I am so glad I am here to see my bestie win it all." Kayla gushed, elated to be there.

In the lobby of the hotel the girls grabbed the key cards from Sardinia's dad and ran ahead of everyone to find their rooms and unlock the doors.

"Look at these elevators!" Sardinia exclaimed. The elevators were made totally of glass, and you could see everything from them. The hotel looked like a palace, and neither of them had ever been in such a place.

After settling into their rooms and dressing for the ceremony, they all left for the Convention Center.

As they entered the dining room, a young girl handed them each a program and led them to their assigned table.

"Wow, we are sitting right up front," her dad uttered with a smile, "I guess we are in the VIP section."

Mrs. Dyer handed Sardinia a manila folder that contained a copy of her story.

"What's this for?" Silk asked.

"All of the teachers were asked to bring a copy of their student's work in case they won the Grand Prize," Mrs. Dyer answered. "Place it under your seat."

After an elaborate dinner of salad, warm rolls, Chicken Cordon Bleu, Strip Steak with mushrooms, mashed potatoes and gravy, asparagus and corn, the Master of Ceremonies, Mrs. Matz, took the stage. She was the CEO of the publishing company and announced that she would be starting the awards ceremony while the waiters cleared the tables and served dessert, cheesecake with strawberries.

Yummy! Silk thought.

"I want to first thank all of you for coming to the ceremony this evening in which we will be highlighting some very special young talent," Mrs. Matz started. "A special thank you to all of the educators and parents for nurturing these gifted writers into the talented young people they have become." Silk watched as everyone rose to their feet and applauded.

"Wow, Silk, this is so nerve racking," Kayla mumbled, squeezing Silk's arm.

"I know. My stomach feels funny," Silk whispered.

"Are you sure it's just nerves and not because you ate two helpings of mashed potatoes and gravy?" Kayla laughed.

"No, it's nerves," Silk answered.

"Tonight, as we announce each teacher's name, we ask that they come up on the stage with their students. Once you get on stage, please tell everyone what school and state you're representing and introduce your award winner. After your introduction, please take a seat on the stage and when everyone is on the stage, we will announce our grand prize winner," Mrs. Matz instructed.

"I didn't know I had to go on stage, Mrs. Dyer," Sardinia **stammered...** *meaning to speak with sudden pauses and repeat the initial letters of words.*

"It's not a big deal, Sardinia. You will be fine," Mrs. Dyer reassured her and patted her hand.

Mrs. Dyer's name was finally called. She leaned over and gave Sardinia a wink.

Sardinia was introduced on stage, and then she and Mrs. Dyer took their places. It was quite a while until all the teachers and their students had all taken their seats, and Silk wondered if everyone's hands were sore from all the clapping they had been doing.

She laughed to herself, feeling a tingle in her own hands.

After a few people spoke about the history of the contest, explained the publishing procedures, and went over the itinerary of the trip to Disney World, the time had finally arrived.

"My hands are sweating," Mrs. Dyer whispered to Sardinia. "Remember even if you don't win, you are already a winner."

"I know this is the moment everyone has been waiting for," Mrs. Matz announced. "We once again would like to tell all of these amazing young people that every one of them has the talent and imagination to continue to expand their writing careers. You are all winners, and I wish we could send you all to Disney, but unfortunately we cannot.

After reading all of these spectacular entries, the Grand Prize Winner of the 12th Annual Keystone Publishing Company's

Contest for Young Writers is..." *the whole convention center was completely quiet as Mrs. Matz continued* "...Jessica Lahr from the Nazareth Intermediate School, Nazareth, Pennsylvania! Congratulations to Jessica and all of our other winners!"

A scream sounded from the audience as the family of the winner was cheering and jumping up and down. Silk looked at Mrs. Dyer and mumbled, "I'm sorry I didn't win."

"Are you kidding? I'm honored just to be here," Mrs. Dyer said. "Without your wonderful imagination, it would have never happened. Keep your head up. I'm so proud of you."

As Silk was exiting the stage, trying to get past the glaring lights, Mrs. Matz beckoned her to the judge's table.

A man dressed in a navy-blue business suit greeted her from behind the table.

"Miss Kingstree, my name is Chester Buss," he said. "I'm the Editor-in-Chief of the Keystone Publishing Company."

Silk was taken aback at being singled out. She did not understand what was going on. Mrs. Dyer doubled back when she noticed Sardinia being summoned to the judge's table with a huge smile on her face.

"We have been given the honor to have previewed your Daily Journal writings," Mr. Buss was saying.

"What?" Sardinia gasped. "How did you get my journal? That was private and I gave that to...." She stretched her neck to find Kayla in the crowd.

"Sardinia," Mrs. Dyer interrupted, "I allowed him look at it."

"But I don't understand," Sardinia babbled, "How did you get it?"

"Kayla shared it with me while we were driving here, and I was so impressed that I asked Mr. Buss to look at it. I am sorry. I should have asked you first, but I was so excited I just had to show him how talented you are," Mrs. Dyer exclaimed apologetically.

"Miss Kingstree," Mr. Buss carried on, "we would love to publish your creative writing in a book of your own. We could also give you the honor of being signed on as a guest junior editor, so you'll be able to learn about the publishing process, help edit, and work alongside our editors, who will be working on your publication. Please consider this offer. After your collection of writings is published, you will be paid for each book that sells, and you will also be able to travel to numerous venues to do book signings. What do you think?"

"What's going on?" Mr. Kingstree interrupted as he had finally trudged his way through the crowd to the judge's table.

"Hello, Mr. Kingstree, my name is Mr. Buss, I am the Editor-in-Chief of the Keystone Publishing Company, and I have just offered your very talented daughter a chance of a lifetime."

Still in a fog and feeling **blindsided...** *meaning to catch someone unprepared*, Silk smiled and hugged her dad.

"Kayla!" Silk yelled. "Thank you, wherever you are!" She wasn't quite sure if Kayla even heard her.

"I would love to have my own book published and do book signings as long as it is okay with my mom and dad," Silk gushed.

"That would be wonderful. We will be in contact with you next week sometime," Mr. Buss congratulated Sardinia by shaking her hand and nodding to Mr. Kingstree.

Finally, Kayla and Mrs. Kingstree joined the small group.

"You aren't mad at me, are you?" Kayla inquired, unsure of how Silk would respond to the sharing of her journal.

"I could never be mad at you," Silk said. "I will forever be grateful for having a friend like you. Most of all, thank you for helping me finally realize and be happy with who I am... Sardinia Louise Kingstree, and that's all.

About the Author

LYNN ANN POST resides between Nazareth, Pennsylvania, and Manning, South Carolina. She lives with her husband, Norman, and has two daughters, Stacy and Jessica. She also has

three grandchildren, Mikaylah and twins, Lena and Kole, all of whom help keep her young. She is the daughter of Elaine Dilliard and the late Melvin Dilliard along with her brother, Chris.

In her spare time since retiring from the Nazareth Area School District in Pennsylvania, Lynn Ann enjoys painting, reading, gardening, fishing, spending time with her family and friends, and of course writing.

She graduated from Nazareth Area High School and continued her education by receiving her Associate Degree in Commercial Art from Northampton Area Community College. After getting married, raising two children, and working years as a graphic artist and a few other jobs, she decided to once again pursue her desire to become a teacher by continuing her education and graduating with her Elementary Education Degree and a BA in Art Education from Cedar Crest and Moravian Colleges. She taught at Holy Family Catholic School, Floyd R. Shafer Elementary School, and then the Nazareth Intermediate School until retiring in 2018.

When I was asked to write about myself and why I decided to write this book, I had to sit back and really think it through. What I realized after I had completed writing this book is that the things Sardinia experiences in the story were some of same situations that I had experienced as a child. I remembered my struggles with reading and trying to understand what I read and feeling inferior to my peers in the classroom. I also remembered being made fun of because of the clothing I wore, because they were not name brand. I finally understood why my fingers flowed so smoothly across the keyboard as I wrote this book: Everything I wrote about I had somehow experienced myself.

As a teacher, I could easily relate to those struggling readers and knew I could help them come to understand that there was nothing wrong with them and that they could be successful with a few changes. The looks on their faces when they were successful was priceless. Helping these students fueled my desire to write each day by journaling my daily classroom experiences, thus, Be Careful What You Wish For.

I would like to thank all my students that I have had the pleasure of teaching throughout the years, but most of all a special thank you to my last class of 2017-2018 for your ideas and suggestions. You educated me and gave me the strength and desire to complete this book. This is for you!

CPSIA information can be obtained
at www.ICGtesting.com
Printed in the USA
LVHW051010110621
689905LV00012B/1784